DENNIS HASELEY

TWENTY HEARTBEATS

Illustrations by
ED YOUNG

A NEAL PORTER BOOK
ROARING BROOK PRESS
NEW YORK

I am indebted to the book Legend, Myth and Magic in the Image of the Artist
by Ernst Kris and Otto Kurz (Yale University Press, 1979) for the anecdote that inspired this story.—D.H.

A Neal Porter Book
Published by Roaring Brook Press
Roaring Brook Press is a division of Holtzbrinck Publishing Holdings Limited Partnership
175 Fifth Avenue, New York, New York 10010
www.roaringbrookpress.com

Distributed in Canada by H. B. Fenn and Company, Ltd.

Library of Congress Cataloging-in-Publication Data
Haseley, Dennis.
Twenty heartbeats / by Dennis Haseley ; illustrated by Ed Young. — 1st ed.
p. cm.
"A Neal Porter book."
Summary: After waiting for decades for the portrait of his prize horse to be finished,
an angry rich man decides to confront the artist.
ISBN-13: 978-1-59643-238-3
ISBN-10: 1-59643-238-1
[1. Artists—Fiction. 2. Horses—Fiction. 3. Painting—Fiction.]
I. Young, Ed, ill.   II. Title.   PZ7.H2688Tw 2008
[E]—dc22

Roaring Brook Press books are available for special promotions and premiums.
For details, contact: Director of Special Markets, Holtzbrinck Publishers.

Designed by Jennifer Browne
Printed in China
First Edition 2008
2 4 6 8 10 9 7 5 3 1

For Claudia
—D.H.

For Antonia, my daughter who loves horses
—E.Y.

A wealthy man
dreamed of a painting
of his favorite horse.
It was the one who always came to him
when he whistled.
He would hang the picture on the wall
that overlooked his lake.

He sought out Homan,
who was known
as a great painter of horses.

So alive were they, real horses whinnied
if they saw them; flies tried to land
on the brushstrokes of their skin.
The man gave Homan
a great bag of gold
in payment for his work.

"Bring the animal to me,"
said Homan.

Homan reached out his hand.
He touched the horse's nose, neck, flank;
then circled back,
tail to head.
"That is enough."

"Enough?
You've hardly looked at him,"
said the man.

"I will call you when it is ready,"
said Homan with a bow.

The wealthy man went on his way,
eager for the painting
of the horse he loved.

A day went by.
A week.

The wealthy man stood on his terrace.
He watched his horse grazing
in the field.
He looked over the lake
and wondered about his painting.
Rains came and went; flowers wilted, others grew.
He sat in a fine chair
and stared at the empty spot on his wall
where the picture would hang.

More weeks went by.
A month.
The horse reared,
the man whistled
and it ran to him
in twenty heartbeats,
tossing its head.

A year went by.
Two.
The trees around the lake
grew taller.
He fed the horse
sweet oats
from his hand.

Three more years went by.
The lake was lower.
The spot on the wall
was faded
from the sunlight.

The man wrote a letter to Homan.
"Have you forgotten my work?"
Another returned:
"I am progressing well."

Three more years went by.
Every day the man waited,
and every day there was
no word from Homan.

The man's hair
began to turn gray.
His beard was longer.
The horse had gray hair, too.
It could no longer
lift itself so high;
when the man whistled,
its gait was slower.

And the trees were taller as well;
they stood high above the lotus blossoms.

Finally the man could wait no longer.
All in a fury, he rushed back to Homan's house.
"Great artist or not,
I cannot last another day!" cried the man.
"I must have the picture of my horse
I paid you for, so many years ago!"
Homan bowed.
"It is almost ready," he said.
"Wait here, please."

The man took a chair.
He began to calm down.
His picture was almost ready.

As he watched, Homan returned
with a blank sheet.

He laid it on a table;
Homan ground colors,
chose brushes.
It took him
twenty heartbeats.

Homan held absolutely still,
staring at the surface.
Then, he made quick strokes
with a large brush.

"Finished at last," said Homan.

The man did not look at the painting.
All he could see were
the years that had gone by.
In anger he cried,
"Years and years have I waited!
And finally, when I come here,
you dash off my picture
like nothing!
They call you a great painter,
but you are the slowest man
I have ever met!"
"I am sorry you feel
that way," said Homan.

He bowed.
He lifted the painting
from the table
and handed it
to the man.

Then Homan turned, and walked into
the shadows of his house,
toward the closed door
of his studio.

The man was so angry
he did not glance
at what he held in his hand.
He followed Homan down the dark hall.
He wanted to say more angry things,
perhaps he wanted his money back . . .

But as the door to Homan's studio opened,
and light entered in,
the man stopped, struck into silence,
and tears sprang to his eyes.

Now he knew what Homan had been struggling with
all those years.

For around him in the bright room—
and down the hall beyond,
as far as his eye could see—

were thousands upon thousands of
paintings of its sweet shape,

one after
the next
trying to capture
what he now held
in his hand:

his horse, rearing, so lifelike . . .
that he whistled to it.